CONNECTIONS READERS

A Family Secret

NINA WEINSTEIN

Series Editor: John Rosenthal

Boston   Burr Ridge, IL   Dubuque, IA   Madison, WI
New York   San Francisco   St. Louis
Bangkok   Bogotá   Caracas   Lisbon   London   Madrid   Mexico City
Milan   New Delhi   Seoul   Singapore   Sydney   Taipei   Toronto

McGraw-Hill

A Division of The **McGraw·Hill** Companies

Connections Readers: A Family Secret

Copyright © 1998 by The McGraw-Hill Companies, Inc.
All rights reserved. Printed in the United States of America.
Except as permitted under the United States Copyright Act of 1976, no part of this publication may be reproduced or distributed in any form or by any means, or stored in a data base or retrieval system, without the prior written permission of the publisher.

This book is printed on acid-free paper.

domestic   1 2 3 4 5 6 7 8 9 0 DOC DOC 9 0 0 9 8 7
international   1 2 3 4 5 6 7 8 9 0 DOC DOC 9 0 0 9 8 7

ISBN 0-07-292792-5

Editorial director: Thalia Dorwick
Publisher: Tim Stookesberry
Development editor: Pam Tiberia
Production supervisor: Tanya Nigh
Print materials consultant: Marilyn Rosenthal
Project manager: Shannon McIntyre, Function Thru Form, Inc.
Design and Electronic Production: Function Thru Form, Inc.
Typeface: Goudy
Printer and Binder: R.R. Donnelley and Sons

Grateful acknowledgment is made for use of the following:
Illustration: © Chris Duke

Library of Congress Catalog Card Number: 97-75582

International Edition

Copyright © 1998. Exclusive rights by The McGraw-Hill Companies, Inc., for manufacture and export. This book cannot be re-exported from the country to which it is consigned by The McGraw-Hill Companies, Inc. The International Edition is not available in North America.

When ordering this title, use ISBN 0-07-115935-5.

http://www.mhhe.com

Chapter 1
The Party

Patrick stood near the bed next to Brendan. The twin bed had dark wood. It matched the rest of the bedroom. The room was barely big enough for two people.

Patrick moved the newspaper on the bed. He didn't look at it. Instead, Patrick picked up a white sock. "Hey," Patrick said, "what's that smell?"

Brendan looked at his younger brother. Patrick was 17 years old, and he only cared about his family and baseball. "Very funny," Brendan said. Brendan was 21. He took the sock from Patrick. "Mom just washed this."

"Where are you going?" Patrick asked. "You've been getting dressed for an hour."

Brendan stood up. He went into the bathroom. The apartment had only one bathroom. Brendan, Patrick, their mother, and their father all used it. Patrick followed him to the bathroom. Patrick had his baseball bat. Brendan got some after-shave from the medicine chest. He put it on his face.

"Oh, you smell nice," Patrick said. "What's so special?"

The Party

Brendan looked at himself in the mirror. He was wearing a white shirt and his father's only dark tie. He put some water on a spot on the tie.

"Look," Brendan said, "there's a party tonight at Sam's house. Rick's going to be there. Jim will be there. Why don't you come?"

Brendan looked at his brother. Patrick wore Brendan's old gray shirt and pants. Patrick smiled. "What would I do at a party?"

Patrick followed Brendan to their room. "You'd talk to people," Brendan said. "You'd eat. Maybe you'd even meet a girl."

Patrick threw his bat to Brendan. Brendan caught it. "We have an important game tomorrow," Patrick said. "The team is depending on me. I have to go to bed early tonight. I can't go to a party."

Brendan put the bat on the bed, next to the newspaper. He turned and watched his younger brother. They were about the same size, but Patrick had always been thinner.

"Don't you care about anything but baseball?" Brendan asked.

"No, not really," Patrick said. He smiled and sat on the bed. He threw the newspaper off the bed.

"Hey, don't do that," Brendan yelled. "I'm still reading that."

"Sorry. What's so important?" Patrick asked.

"There's a story about the war in Korea."

"Korea? That's so far away. Why do you care?" Patrick asked.

Brendan trusted his brother more than anyone. But Patrick sometimes surprised him. "Don't you read the papers?" he asked. "America might be getting into the war. And guys like you and me will have to fight."

"Not me," Patrick said. "I'm too young."

"Fine. Guys like me," Brendan said. "And Sam, and Jim, and a lot of your friends. And a lot of the guys at the party tonight."

Brendan turned to Patrick. He looked serious. "I'll ask one more time," Brendan said. "Will you come to the party?"

Patrick took the bat from the bed and put it under his arm. "No, thanks," he said. "I'd rather talk about baseball than about war."

Brendan walked across the room. "You lost your chance." Then he left.

Patrick picked up the newspaper and began to read: *U.S. will send 500,000 men to Korea.*

Suddenly Patrick was worried about his older brother. Very worried.

* * *

The Party

Brendan drove through Boston. The party was at an old small house near the Charles River. Brendan loved the Charles River. He and Patrick often walked along the river with their friends on weekends. They would talk about girls and baseball . . . and girls.

Brendan parked his father's old black car. His father was so proud of that car. He came to the United States from Ireland with nothing. He was a very strong man. Now he had a car and a good job at a shipyard. Brendan worked in the shipyard, too, next to his father. It was hard work.

Brendan walked up to the house. He could hear people talking from the street. He could hear music.

He rang the doorbell. Rick answered the door. Rick wore a blue shirt and dark pants. "Hey," Rick said, "where's Patrick?"

"He has a baseball game tomorrow," Brendan said.

"Oh," Rick said.

"He's really good," Brendan said. "He's very serious about baseball." Brendan walked into the small living room. Groups of people were talking. A few people were dancing to a slow song. Brendan saw Jim. He went to an old brown sofa and sat next to him. Jim put his hand on Brendan's back. Jim was a little older than Brendan. He had dark hair and blue eyes. He also worked in the shipyard.

"There are sandwiches and drinks on the table," Jim said.

"No, thanks. I'm not hungry," Brendan said.

"Hey, you look serious. What's wrong?"

"I don't know," Brendan said. "What do you think about Korea?" Every young man was thinking about the Korean War.

Jim put his hands into his pockets. "We have to keep the world free," he said. "For our women and children."

"Your dad told you that," Brendan said. "Do you really believe that?"

"I don't know. But if we have to go to war, then we have to go. We don't really have a choice."

Brendan combed his fingers through his short hair. "Yeah, you're right," he said to Jim.

Suddenly Brendan stood up. He saw a young woman by the door. She had wavy dark hair and dark eyes. She looked so happy, almost like a child. She was beautiful.

"Who is that?" Brendan asked.

"Molly Kelly's little sister," Jim said. "I think her name is Margaret."

"Introduce me," Brendan said to Jim.

The Party

"No," Jim said. "She's just a kid. She's only 16 or 17."

"She looks older," Brendan said. "Introduce me," he repeated.

"All right!" Jim said. "All right. But I barely know her."

Brendan watched the young woman. She was talking to a group of people. She laughed easily and often. They walked past Sam. Sam put his hand on Brendan's arm. "Hey, I want to tell you something."

"Later," Brendan said. He couldn't stop watching the young woman. She looked like she loved life. Brendan and Jim stopped in front of her.

"Margaret?" Jim said. "I want you to meet someone. Margaret Kelly, this is Brendan Casey."

She looked directly at Brendan. "Casey is it? Would you be Irish?"

"I would," Brendan said. "My parents are from Galway, Ireland."

"I don't believe it. My family is from Ballinrobe, Ireland."

"We were almost neighbors," Brendan said. "Would you . . . would you like something to eat?"

"Yes, I would. Thank you," she said. "Let me tell my sister. I don't want her to worry about me."

Margaret walked up to a woman with brown hair. She was maybe 21 or 22. She had the same dark eyes as Margaret.

Brendan got their food. He sat on the sofa. He watched Margaret walk, and he watched her talk. She said hello to a few people as she walked across the room.

Brendan gave Margaret her sandwich and a drink. Margaret told him she wanted to be a singer.

He worked in a shipyard. He couldn't believe it. He met a beautiful young woman who wanted to be a singer. He couldn't think about anything else.

Chapter 2
The Letter

Weeks later, Brendan was having a dream, a beautiful dream. In the dream, Margaret Kelly wore all white. She was singing in a big building. It was night. There were over a thousand seats, but she was singing only to him. Suddenly, he heard bells. He wanted the bells to stop.

"Hey, Brendan!"

Brendan opened his eyes. He saw Patrick.

"Hey, Brendan," Patrick said. "Get up. Sam's on the phone. He sounds . . . strange."

Brendan got up and went to the kitchen. He picked up the phone. "Hi," he said.

"What took you so long?" Sam said.

"I don't know," Brendan said. "What's going on?"

Sam cleared his throat. "I got it."

"You got what?" Brendan said. Brendan's mother was working in the kitchen. She was a short, strong-looking woman with black hair. His mother and father had met in 1920 on the way to the United States. They were both Irish. They came with just their clothes and a small amount of money. They made a life here. Sometimes their life was hard.

5

The Letter

His mother put an egg into a frying pan. Brendan listened to the sound of the egg cooking.

"I got my notice," Sam said. "I have to go into the army."

Brendan felt like he'd been hit in the stomach. "When?" he asked his best friend.

"Immediately."

Later that afternoon, Brendan and Patrick went to a park near their apartment. They both wore old shirts and pants. It was a small park with a basketball court.

Patrick had the ball. He ran across the court. Brendan was close behind him. Patrick shot the ball. It went into the basket.

Brendan got the ball. Patrick was next to him. Brendan tried to shoot, but Patrick put his arm up. Brendan tried again. Patrick stood next to the basket. Brendan shot. He missed.

Brendan didn't like to lose, and he hated to lose to Patrick. They'd been that way since they were small.

Patrick got the ball. He shot. He made the basket again.

Brendan got the ball. He shot again. He almost made it, but he missed again.

Brendan took the ball. He walked away from the court.

Patrick ran up to him. They were both breathing hard. "Hey, I'm sorry. I tried too hard to win. We both want the same things, I guess."

Brendan stopped at a small grassy field. They used to play baseball on this field when they were small.

"What's wrong with you?" Patrick said. "You've been angry at me all day. Are you having a problem with Margaret?"

"No. It's not Margaret. She's great. Did I tell you she wants to be a singer?"

"Only about a hundred times," Patrick said. "So if it's not her, what is it?"

Brendan sat down on the grass. He said nothing.

Patrick sat next to his brother. "You've been angry since the phone call from Sam. What did he say to you?"

Brendan couldn't look at his brother. He pulled out some grass and threw it into the air. "Sam's leaving," Brendan said. "He's going into the army."

Patrick put his hand on Brendan's arm. "I'm sorry."

Brendan stood. There was a strong breeze. He shook his head. He put his hands into his pockets. Their father taught them not to talk about their feelings. He said that a real man didn't talk about his feelings. He turned away from Patrick.

The Letter

Patrick watched his brother. Patrick didn't like talking about feelings, either. But he knew Brendan was upset. He pushed his older brother.

"Stop playing around," Brendan said. He was very serious.

"Come on," Patrick said. "Let's play another game. I'll let you win."

"No. It's getting late. I'm going out with Margaret tonight," Brendan said. "Let's go home."

Patrick knew about Brendan's date, but he acted surprised. "You're going to let a woman come between us? I don't believe it."

"She's prettier than you are," Brendan said.

Brendan and Patrick walked to their apartment on Blossom Street. The street was mostly apartment buildings. Many of them were old and gray. Some were painted bright colors. Most had three or four floors and a small square of grass.

Their apartment was in an old white building with three floors. It was on the top floor. Brendan and Patrick opened the door to their building. The hall was dark.

The mailman was walking to the mailboxes. He was probably 40 years old. His name was Harry. He always wore a hat and a mailman's jacket. His pants were always too big.

Harry took off his hat. He handed a thin letter to Brendan. "I think this is for you," he said.

Brendan took the letter. The mailman left. He and Patrick sat on the stairs of their apartment building. Brendan looked at the letter for a long time.

"Don't open it," Patrick said.

"That won't change it," Brendan said.

Brendan tore open the letter.

"What does it say?" Patrick said.

"I have to go," Brendan said. "I have to go into the army."

Patrick's eyes were wide. He was never afraid, but he looked afraid now. He was worried about Brendan. Patrick shook his head. "When?" he said.

"Two weeks."

"Will you have to fight in the war?" Patrick asked.

"I don't know."

Chapter 3
Brother's Keeper

That night, Brendan and Margaret went to a movie. Brendan paid for the tickets. Then he and Margaret went inside. He bought popcorn and two sodas. Then they looked for seats.

"Where do you like to sit?" he asked.

"Let's sit in the back," Margaret said. "There aren't so many people there. We can be alone."

Brendan smiled at her. They found seats in the back.

Brendan sat next to Margaret in the dark. He put his arm around her. Margaret looked at Brendan, but she didn't move away from him. At the end of the movie, Margaret cried.

Brendan and Margaret walked out of the movie. They walked along the sidewalk. There were shoe stores, furniture stores, clothing stores, and restaurants.

Brendan was thinking about the war. "War changed people's lives," he thought. He couldn't tell Margaret about the army yet. He didn't want to lose her.

"Did you like the movie?" Brendan said. He was watching Margaret. She wore a pink blouse and skirt and a white sweater. Her dark hair looked soft against the pink and white clothes.

"It was so sad," Margaret said. "He loved her, but he let her go."
"That's silly," Brendan said. "If they love each other, they should be together."

"It wasn't that easy. There was a war," she said. "War makes things different."

They walked past a coffee shop. "Are you hungry?" Brendan said.

"I'm always hungry," Margaret said.

They went inside. They sat by a window. They ordered coffee and sandwiches.

Margaret began to eat her sandwich. He watched her eat. He picked up his sandwich. He'd never been this nervous around anyone. He couldn't eat.

"Hey, Margaret," Brendan said, "what did your family do in Ballinrobe?"

"They had a farm," Margaret said. "They couldn't make enough money to live. So they came to the United States."

"My family had a farm, too. A dairy farm," Brendan said. He put his sandwich down. "Wouldn't that be great? Living on a farm? With all the cows and sheep and chickens? You could grow your own food and drink fresh milk every day."

Margaret laughed. "Who would I sing to? The cows or the sheep?"

Brendan laughed, too. His parents had worked so hard to get away from the farm. What was he thinking? He shouldn't have silly dreams like that.

Margaret put down her sandwich. Brendan took her hand. It felt wonderful to sit in the restaurant, holding her hand. They stayed in the restaurant for hours.

* * *

The next day was Sunday. Brendan got up early. He showered and got dressed quickly. He and Margaret were going to take a walk on the beach.

Brendan rushed to the kitchen. He looked in the refrigerator. He put some milk in a glass and drank it.

His mother was cooking something at the stove. "Put it in the sink," she said.

Brendan put the glass in the sink.

His father was sitting at the table. He was wearing a T-shirt and dark pants. His brown hair was thick and uncombed. He was reading the newspaper.

"How did you sleep?" his mother said to Brendan.

"Great," Brendan said.

"What do you want for breakfast?" his mother said.

"No time," Brendan said. "I'm taking Margaret to the beach." He walked to the door.

His father looked up. "Again? You just saw her last night," his father said. He held up the newspaper. "Hey, here's another story about Korea. Don't you want to read it, son?"

Brendan's father was proud of him. A man fought for his country, his father believed. His father didn't say it, but Brendan knew. Brendan wanted to forget about the war. "Can I borrow the car, Dad?"

"Sure," his father said. He threw the keys to Brendan. Brendan caught them with one hand and ran out of the apartment.

* * *

Brendan and Margaret drove to the beach. They laughed and laughed during the drive.

It was a cool day, so there weren't many people on the beach. Brendan could smell the salt in the cold air. They walked on the sand. The ocean looked gray. They sat and watched the waves.

Margaret was wearing only a thin blouse. After a while, she started to shake. Brendan put his arm around her.

"You're cold," he said. "I'm sorry. It was a stupid idea to come here."

"No," Margaret said. "I love it." She rested her head on his shoulder. Suddenly she began to sing:

"Our life's a dream. We barely know we're dreaming."

"Where did you learn that song?" Brendan said when she finished.

"I . . . I wrote it," she said. "It's a lullaby. I wrote it for my five-year-old cousin. Sometimes she can't fall asleep. But I sing the song, and she goes to sleep immediately."

"You have a beautiful voice, and you're beautiful," Brendan said. "Actually, you're perfect."

Margaret laughed. "I'm only perfect to you."

Brendan kissed her. Then he touched her face. "I love you, Margaret Kelly."

"I love you, too," she said.

When Brendan came home, he felt like he was in a dream. He walked into the building, but he didn't remember doing it. He walked up the stairs, but he didn't remember doing that, either. He opened the door to their apartment and walked into the kitchen. Patrick was sitting at the kitchen table.

"What's wrong with you?" Patrick said. "You look like you're not really here."

"I'm not," Brendan said.

Brendan sat across from his brother. He put his feet on a chair and his elbows on the table. "I was with Margaret."

"Again? You just saw her last night," Patrick said.

"I know. She's really special. I think she could be the future Mrs. Casey."

"Excuse me?" Patrick said. He was surprised. "You really like her."

"Yeah, I really do."

"Have you told her about the army yet?"

"No, not yet," Brendan said

"Well, what are you waiting for? You leave a week from Monday."

"I'm going to tell her next Saturday. I'm planning a big night."

Brendan turned to his brother. "Patrick, I need you to do something for me."

"I'll do anything for you," Patrick said. "You know that." Brendan looked at him. Patrick seemed sad. Brendan was going to miss him terribly.

"I trust you more than anyone," Brendan said. "Promise that you'll take care of her. I need you to take care of Margaret."

"Take care of her? What do you mean?"

"Talk to her, take her to the movies, have lunch with her. Take her to your baseball games. Just be with her until I get back from the war."

"You mean go out with her, like a date?"

"It won't be like a date. You're my brother. Just don't let anybody else go on dates with her. When I come home, I'm going to marry her."

Chapter 4
The Last Night

Brendan rushed from the bathroom to his bedroom. He was still a little wet. He dropped his towel on the floor and started getting dressed. He put on a purple sweater and black pants. The sweater was Patrick's. Brendan stood at the mirror.

His father walked in. He looked at Brendan. "You must be joking."

Brendan turned to his father. "Really? Do I look that bad?"

"Worse." His father left. He came back with a dark suit. "Look," his father said, "why don't you borrow this?"

His father held the suit up. It was his only suit. "Dad, I don't know. What if I get something on it?"

"You're going out with Margaret," his father said.

"Yeah," Brendan said.

"Then you need the suit." Brendan's father put the suit on the bed.

"Thanks, Dad," Brendan said.

Brendan put on the suit. He came downstairs. Patrick was standing next to the refrigerator.

"You look . . . not bad. Actually, you look pretty good. Are you going out with Margaret?" Patrick said.

The Last Night

"What do you think?" Brendan said. Brendan went to the refrigerator. He took the milk and drank it from the bottle.

Patrick sat at the table. "So tonight's the big night. You're going to tell her tonight?" He looked serious.

"Yeah. At dinner," Brendan said.

* * *

Brendan took Margaret to a restaurant. They sat at a table for two in a corner of the restaurant. The restaurant was near the center of Boston. They could see the city lights from their window. They were sitting, alone. It felt like they were in a dream together.

"More salt for your steak?" Brendan asked. He was nervous.

"No, thank you," she said.

Brendan put down the salt. He watched her. She wore a black dress with no jewelry. Her hair was up. She looked beautiful.

"Pepper?" Brendan said.

"No, thanks, Brendan," Margaret said. She smiled at him. "My steak is fine. It's perfect. This whole evening is so wonderful. What's the big occasion?"

Brendan felt happier than he'd ever been. And sadder. He couldn't look at her. He kept eating his steak.

"Something's wrong," she said. "I can feel it."

Margaret stopped eating and looked up at him. Her fork made a loud noise when she dropped it on the plate. Finally, Brendan looked up at her. He reached his hand across the table and held Margaret's hand. "I couldn't tell you before," he said.

"Tell me what?"

"I'm leaving."

"Leaving?" she asked. "What are you talking about?"

"I got my notice. I'm going into the army. I have six weeks of practice, then I get my assignment. I leave Monday. I'm sorry."

Margaret was shocked. "Monday! Why didn't you tell me before?"

"I couldn't," Brendan said. There were tears in his eyes, but he was not crying. "I don't want to leave you, but I have to." He cleared the tears from his eyes. "I have to ask you something. I'll understand if you say no, but I have to ask you."

"What is it, Brendan?"

"I . . . I want you to wait for me. I want us to be together. I need you in my life."

Margaret turned to him. Now there were tears on her face. "I'll wait."

* * *

The Last Night

On Monday, Patrick, his father, and his mother took Brendan to the bus station. There were other families saying goodbye to their sons, but Brendan didn't notice them. Brendan thought about the war. "I might have to go to Korea. I might have to shoot someone. Someone might shoot me. I might never see Margaret or Patrick or Mom and Dad again."

His mother wore a green dress. It was the same dress she wore to church. She gave Patrick a package. "Here's some food," she said. "If you get hungry."

His father shook Brendan's hand. "I'm . . . I'm . . . proud of you, son," he said. Then his father turned away from him.

Patrick wore a T-shirt under his jacket. He looked so much like a kid, but he wasn't. He was bigger than Brendan. "When did Patrick become a man?" Brendan wondered.

Patrick looked directly into Brendan's eyes. "Be careful," Patrick said. Then he hugged his brother.

"Take care of Margaret," Brendan said into Patrick's ear. "She's the most important thing in my life."

* * *

Margaret sat alone in her small bedroom. "Will Brendan be safe?" she wondered. "When will I ever see him again?"

She tried to read, but she couldn't think. She tried to sew, but she kept making mistakes. She sang, but even that didn't make her happy. It was almost dark.

She heard someone at the door. "Who is it?" she said.

It was her sister, Molly. "You've been in there for hours," Molly said. "Can I come in?"

Margaret cleaned the tears from her face. She got up from the bed and opened the door.

Molly stood in the middle of the room for a minute and looked at Margaret. Molly was almost five years older than Margaret. She had dark hair. She wore a white blouse, a brown sweater, and a brown skirt. She was thin, and a little shorter than Margaret. She loved to watch Margaret sing. She loved to watch Margaret go out. She seemed to think of Margaret's dreams as her own.

Molly walked to a chair by the bed. She sat. "It's been four weeks," Molly said.

"What?" Margaret said.

"Brendan left four weeks ago. You only leave this room to go to school. You never see any friends. You have to leave this room."

The Last Night

"I . . . I can't," Margaret said.

Molly put her hands on Margaret's shoulders and shook her gently. "I'm worried about you."

"I'm fine."

"What about Patrick?"

"Who?" Margaret said.

"Patrick," Molly said. "Brendan's brother."

"What about him?" Margaret said.

"He called again," Molly said.

Margaret got up. She went to the window.

"Please listen," Molly said.

Margaret shook her head. "I'm listening," Margaret said.

"Brendan wants Patrick to take care of you," Molly said. "Patrick told me that. He sounds so sweet."

"That's very nice, but he doesn't understand. Nobody understands."

"Patrick wants to take you to a party," Molly said. "He's Brendan's brother. He's just trying to be your friend."

"I appreciate it," Margaret said. She was still looking out of the window. "Maybe next time."

Molly stood. She went to the window. She put a hand on Margaret's back. The sisters looked at each other. "You sit in this room for hours every day," Molly said. "You think about Brendan and you cry until you fall asleep."

"You knew that?" Margaret asked.

"Everybody in this house knows that," Molly said. "You need to get out of the house and do something fun."

"All right," Margaret said. "I'll go to the party with Patrick."

"You won't be sorry," Molly said.

Chapter 5
Brendan's Girl

Patrick looked in his closet for something to wear. He went into his parents' room. His father was wearing a T-shirt. He was resting on the bed. "Dad, can I borrow your suit?"

"Why?" his father asked.

"I'm going to a party."

"You don't usually wear my suit to parties."

Patrick put his hands into the air. "Brendan asked me to take care of Margaret. I'm taking her to a party."

His father looked at Patrick. He went to the closet. He handed him the suit. "Be careful," his father said.

"I'm not going to war," Patrick said. "I'm just going to a party."

"Just be careful," his father said. Then he shook his head.

"Dad?" Patrick said.

"Yeah. What?"

"Can I borrow the car?"

"Anything else?" his father said.

"No," Patrick said. "That's it."

Patrick drove his father's car to Margaret's apartment. She lived in

16

Brendan's Girl

an apartment on Armstrong Street. It was about half a mile from Patrick's apartment.

He parked his father's big old car. He walked up the walkway and into the building. Girls made him nervous. "Margaret isn't really a girl," Patrick thought. "She's Brendan's girl." This wasn't a date. They were just friends. This would be like going to the movies with a friend.

He rang the doorbell to Apartment 5. A young woman answered the door. She looked like Margaret. She had dark hair and dark eyes, but she seemed so . . . old. She was probably at least 21 or 22.

"You must be Patrick," she said. "Come in. I'll get Margaret."

She walked with Patrick into the living room. He waited while she went to get Margaret. He didn't feel comfortable in his suit. He put his hands into his pockets. Another woman came in. She was much older. She was obviously Margaret's mother.

"Hello," she said. "I'm Mrs. Kelly. Margaret will be ready in a minute."

"Oh," Patrick said. He didn't know what to say. He looked at his shoes. "Thank you," he said nervously.

Finally, Margaret rushed into the living room. Patrick had never seen her before. She wore a red-and-white dress, and she held a white purse. She had dark hair and dark eyes.

"Hi," she said. She was nervous, but she tried to act calm. "You look like Brendan. I'm Margaret Kelly. That's my sister, Molly." She pointed to the woman who had answered the door. "You've already met my mother. You must be Patrick Casey."

Patrick kept looking at Margaret.

"What?" Margaret said. "Is something wrong with my face?"

"No, no," Patrick said. "Your face is . . . fine." He wanted to say "beautiful." "She's incredible," Patrick thought. "Now I know why Brendan likes her so much."

Margaret turned to her mother. "We'll be back early."

"Have a good time," Mrs. Kelly said.

They left Margaret's apartment. They walked out of the building and down the sidewalk. Patrick pointed to the left. "My car's over there," he said.

"That's Brendan's car. Did he give it to you?" Margaret asked.

"Actually, it's our dad's car. He lets us borrow it."

Patrick and Margaret didn't talk in the car. Patrick drove to Jim's apartment and parked the car. He got out and opened the car door for Margaret. She gave him her hand. Patrick didn't know what to do.

"Should I take her hand?" he thought. He tried not to look at her. Finally, Margaret got out of the car by herself.

Patrick heard some music. It was coming from Jim's apartment building. Patrick and Margaret walked into the building and went upstairs. Still they didn't say anything.

The apartment door was open. Patrick and Margaret walked in. There was a big gray sofa in the middle of the room and chairs everywhere. There must have been 50 people in the small room. Patrick looked at Margaret. She seemed a little uncomfortable. Patrick felt uncomfortable, too.

Patrick saw Jim. His dark hair was still wet. He shook Patrick's hand. His eyes looked very blue in the blue-gray room. Jim looked at Margaret.

"Have you gotten any letters from Brendan?" Jim said to her.

"Twice a week," she said softly.

Rick walked over to them. He combed his fingers through his short, light brown hair. He and Brendan had been friends for 15 years. "Isn't that Brendan's suit?" Rick said to Patrick.

"It's my dad's suit," Patrick said

"There's food and sodas in the kitchen," Jim said. "Help yourself."

Jim walked over to his girlfriend. She had dark hair and green eyes. A slow song was playing. Jim and his girlfriend started dancing.

Margaret looked around. Young men and women were dancing slowly. Some of them were hugging and kissing. She turned to Patrick. "Maybe this was a bad idea," she said. "Can you take me home?"

"What's the matter?" Patrick said.

"I don't know," she said. "Maybe we shouldn't be here."

Patrick walked with her to the sofa. "We're here now. Why don't we stay a little longer? Then, if you still want to go, I'll take you home."

Margaret let out a deep breath. "OK," she said. She sat on the sofa.

Patrick got two sodas from the kitchen. When he saw Margaret again, he felt so good. "What's wrong with me?" he thought. "Margaret is my brother's girlfriend. I shouldn't think of her like that."

He gave Margaret her soda. He didn't understand his feelings. "Maybe you're right. Maybe we should go," Patrick said. "I have a baseball game tomorrow."

"You play baseball?" Margaret said.

"Yes."

"I love baseball," she said.

"You love to watch?"

"I love to play," Margaret said. "I play for my high school team. It's an all-girls school. We have girls' baseball games."

"Girls' baseball isn't really baseball," Patrick said.

"Why not?"

"Because you're girls."

"Then what is it?"

"I don't know," Patrick said, "but it isn't baseball."

"I'm a catcher," Margaret said. "A good catcher. My father wanted boys, but he got girls. He taught me to play."

"I don't believe it," Patrick said.

"The party was a bad idea," Patrick thought. There were too many of Brendan's friends. It made them sad. They both missed Brendan.

"Let's get out of here," Patrick said.

"I agree," Margaret said. They walked outside. Patrick drove her home. Again, they didn't talk in the car. They walked together to the front of Margaret's apartment. Patrick stopped walking and put his hands in his pockets.

"Do you think about Brendan a lot?" he asked.

"All of the time," she said. "But I can't talk to anybody about it. My parents don't really know him."

"Um, you can . . . you can talk to me about it," Patrick said. "If you want."

"Thanks, Patrick. That's sweet. Hey, do you really have a baseball game tomorrow?" she asked. "Or did you just say that so we could leave."

"I just said that. My game's on Tuesday."

"Can I come and watch? Maybe I can give you some advice about the game."

Patrick laughed. He wasn't nervous anymore. "Sure. Maybe I'll pitch to you after the game."

"OK. I'll see you Tuesday. And thanks, Patrick. I had a nice time."

Patrick said goodbye and drove home. He felt better. He was keeping his promise to Brendan, but it was easy. He was taking care of Margaret, but she was like a friend.

"She's just like my guy friends," he thought.

Chapter 6
Brendan Goes to Korea

After school on Tuesday, Patrick went to the baseball field. He saw Margaret there. She was sitting with a small crowd, waiting. Patrick walked onto the field and stood behind home plate. He was the catcher.

Patrick's team played well. Patrick got two hits. His team won, 7 to 3.

After the game, Margaret walked over to Patrick. She was wearing a pink cotton dress and white tennis shoes.

"Good game," she said.

Patrick rested the bat on his shoulder. "Do you really think so?" he said.

She took the bat from him. "Why don't you throw me some balls?" she said.

Patrick watched her. She was thin and didn't look very strong. But she held the bat perfectly. He backed up a little. He tried to throw the ball softly.

She put down the bat. She looked angry. "You throw like a girl," she said. "Throw it right."

Patrick threw the ball harder.

He heard a sharp sound as the bat hit the ball. Patrick quickly

Brendan Goes to Korea

turned and watched the ball. It kept going and going. She had slammed it to the end of the field.

Patrick's hands fell to his sides. He couldn't believe it. He shook his head.

"Hey!" she shouted. "Go get the ball! Throw me another one."

Patrick didn't know what to say. He didn't know any girls who played baseball. Patrick ran and got the ball.

"I'm ready," she said.

He threw the ball again and again. She kept hitting it to the end of the field. He'd never had this much fun with a girl.

* * *

When Margaret came home from Patrick's baseball game, the mailman was there. He had been their mailman for many years. He handed Margaret a letter.

"It looks important," the mailman said. He gave her two other letters for her father.

Margaret watched the mailman leave. She looked at the the name and address on the outside of the letter. It was from Brendan. When the mailman left, Margaret tore open the white envelope. She opened the letter and began to read.

Dear Margaret,

I miss you so much. We're working very hard here. We get up every morning at 5:00 A.M.

Everything is happening so fast. Margaret, I don't know how to tell you this. I got my assignment. I'm going to Korea. Please tell Patrick and my parents. I don't have time to write to them. It's very important.

I love you.
Brendan

Margaret put down the letter. Her legs felt weak. A cold breeze blew through the trees near the street. She put the letter into her jacket pocket.

She walked down Armstrong Street. She began to run. She ran to Patrick and Brendan's building.

She rushed up the stairs and rang the doorbell to their apartment.

Patrick opened the door. He had just showered. He was wearing a white shirt, dark blue pants, and no shoes. He was surprised to see Margaret. His father was at work, and his mother was shopping.

"Come in," Patrick said.

Brendan Goes to Korea

She came in, but she didn't sit. Margaret showed him the letter. He looked at the envelope. She walked to the window while Patrick read the letter. She turned to Patrick. "He got his assignment."

"Why didn't we . . . ?"

"He didn't have time to write to both of us," she said. "He wanted me to tell you."

"Where is he . . . ?"

"Korea," she said.

Patrick felt like someone had hit him in the stomach.

Margaret didn't want to cry. But when she looked at Patrick, she couldn't stop. The tears fell down her face.

"Patrick, I'm so worried about Brendan," she said. "What if something happens to him? What if he dies?"

He went to Margaret. They stood at the edge of the room. They looked at each other. He felt tears in his eyes, but he didn't cry. He wanted to be strong for Margaret. He put his arms around her.

Her arms and her back felt strong, and yet soft. Patrick held the letter in one hand. She cried loudly into his shoulder. Finally he moved back a little.

He cleaned the tears from her face with his other hand. Her skin felt soft and warm. He had never touched a woman like this. He had never held a woman before.

She looked at him. Her face looked so hurt. His face got closer to hers. He wanted to kiss her.

"What am I doing?" he thought. "She's my brother's girlfriend. I can't do this. I love my brother. He trusted me."

Suddenly, he let Margaret go. He walked to the other side of the room.

Margaret looked embarrassed. She cleared the tears from her eyes again. Then she shook her head. "I'll . . . I'll go now."

Chapter 7
Help Around the House

Margaret sat on the steps to her apartment building with her sister, Molly. The sun was out, but it was a cold day. The trees blew in the strong breeze. She was wearing an old blue sweater and black pants. She was waiting for the mailman.

"What happened with Patrick?" Molly said. "He never calls anymore. You stay in your room and sing all day. I hear you crying at night. I'm worried about you."

Margaret thought about Patrick every day. "Why do I feel so close to him?" she wondered. "I can't believe it. We almost kissed. This is totally wrong."

"Nothing happened," Margaret said. "Patrick's just . . . busy."

"You're afraid of something," Molly said. "I know it."

Neither of them heard the mailman. When Margaret looked up, he was standing next to Molly. He had a letter in his hand.

"This is for you," he said to Margaret.

Margaret took the letter. She looked at the address on the envelope. It was from Brendan. It was his first letter from Korea.

The mailman went inside the building. Molly stood up and started to go inside, too.

Help Around the House

Margaret put a hand on her arm. "Don't go," she said.

Molly sat down. She put her arm around her sister. Margaret sat closer to her sister. Margaret started to read the letter to herself.

* * *

Patrick wanted to be busy every minute. He didn't want to think about Margaret. "I almost kissed her," he thought. "I can't kiss my brother's girlfriend. What's wrong with me? Brendan trusted me to keep other guys away from his girl. But I can't stop thinking about her. I want to be with her."

Patrick saw his mother carrying bags of food into the apartment. He walked over to her.

"Here, Mom, " he said. He took three bags of food. "Let me do that."

He carried the food into the kitchen, then he put it away.

"Thank you," she said. "That's very helpful."

"Mom," Patrick said, "I want to do more around here." He put the empty bags under the sink.

His mother walked to the sink. She stopped next to Patrick. "More?" she said.

"Yes. Aren't there some things I could do? I don't know. Things Brendan used to do?"

"Are you OK?" She put her hand on his forehead.

"I'm fine. I don't have a temperature," Patrick said. "I just want to help you."

"Well, sure. You can clean the floors. Brendan used to do that every Saturday. Or you can clean the bathroom. It's always dirty." His mother sat on a chair in the kitchen and brushed her hands against her old cotton dress. "You know, you don't have to take Brendan's place. Brendan will be home from the war soon. Then everything will be the way it was."

Patrick put his hands into the air. "What's wrong with everyone? I'm just trying to help."

"Nothing," his mother said. "I just . . ."

Patrick rushed to the door. He slammed it behind him.

* * *

Margaret finished reading the letter. She moved away from Molly.

"What happened?" Molly said. "What did the letter say?"

Margaret stood up. She felt like she had done something wrong. "Why do I feel this way?" she thought. "I didn't do anything wrong. I need to see Patrick. I have to tell him we didn't do anything wrong. I have to tell him we're just friends."

"I have to go," Margaret said to Molly. "I have to show this letter to Patrick."

"Why? What's in the letter?"

Margaret rushed down the street.

"Margaret!" Molly shouted.

Molly ran after her. Molly took her sister's arm. "Stop," Molly said. "Stop this right now! What's going on?"

Margaret showed her the letter. Molly stood at the edge of the street, reading:

Dear Margaret,

I'm in Korea. My new address is on the envelope. I miss you so much.

I'm glad Patrick is taking care of you. I don't want you to be alone. I don't want to lose you to another guy. But you're safe with Patrick.

I saw a man die yesterday. He was standing next to me. There was an explosion. He pushed me away from the explosion. And he died.

I wrote a letter to his mother. I didn't know what to say. I said she should be proud of her son. Then I cried.

Margaret, I love you.
Brendan

"This is awful," Margaret said. "Explosions? People dying? Poor Brendan."

Molly put her hands on Margaret's shoulders. "Calm down." She held her sister.

Margaret backed away. "I don't know what to do," Margaret said. She was on the other side of the street now. She put the letter into her pocket. "I have to see Patrick. I have to show him this letter."

"That's a good idea," Molly said. "He'll help you understand your feelings."

Margaret rushed down the street.

"I have no feelings for Patrick," she kept telling herself. "I love Brendan," she thought. She ran up the stairs to Patrick's apartment building. She rang his doorbell.

Patrick opened the door. He had a bucket in his hand. He wore a T-shirt and pants. He looked at her, but he didn't say anything.

Margaret's stomach felt sick. Patrick's face looked so gentle. Her feelings for him rushed at her. They felt a lot like her feelings for Brendan, but that couldn't be. She got angry at herself. "What's wrong with me?" she wondered. "Am I feeling love for Brendan or for Patrick? I thought I loved Brendan, but I keep thinking about Patrick. Could my love for Brendan disappear?" She put her hands into her pockets.

"May I come in?" she said to Patrick.

Patrick put down the bucket. He was happy to see her, but he was afraid, too. He didn't want to be alone with Margaret. "I was washing the floors," he said. "Maybe we should talk outside."

Patrick walked into the dark hall with Margaret. She rested her shoulders against the wall. Her dark hair fell into her eyes. There were tears in her eyes. Patrick wanted to touch her so much. He was angry at himself. He wanted to put his arms around her, but he couldn't.

"What do you want?" he asked.

"Why are you so angry?" Margaret said.

"I'm not angry," Patrick said. He let out a deep breath. "Why are you here?"

"We didn't do anything wrong," she said.

"Of course not," Patrick said. "Who said we did something wrong?"

Margaret showed him the letter. He read it. Then he read it again. Patrick put a hand on the wall. He shook his head.

"Go," Patrick said. "Please. Just go."

Margaret took the letter and left.

Chapter 8
A Surprise Meeting

Margaret decided not to see Patrick again. She didn't see him for months. But it felt like a year. The biggest dance of the year was in two weeks. "It's my prom," Margaret thought. "They want me to sing at the prom, but I don't have a date."

Margaret got home from school at 3:00 P.M. Her mother was cleaning the kitchen. Her mother was a thin woman with long black hair. She always put her hair up when she cleaned. She was wearing her work dress, a black cotton dress with a big skirt.

"Hi," her mother said.

Margaret put her books on the table. She felt bad. She kept telling herself, "I don't care about Patrick. I don't care about Patrick." But she still thought about him every day. "I love Brendan," she kept telling herself. But she knew it wasn't true. She tried to think about Brendan, but she could only think about Patrick. She didn't want anyone to see her. "I'm going upstairs," Margaret said.

Her mother looked worried. She always looked worried. "Margaret needs to get out of the house," she thought. "She needs to go outside and see her friends."

27

A Surprise Meeting

"Honey, could you do something for me?" Mrs. Kelly asked. Her hands were wet and soapy.

"All right," Margaret said.

"Can you go to the market for me?" her mother said. "I need some chicken for dinner and some other things. Here's a list, and here's some money."

"Maybe she'll see some friends at the market," her mother thought. "It's better than staying in her room all day."

Margaret took the list and the money. She walked to Harvey's Market on the corner. It was a small red-and-white store. The market had been on their corner for over 30 years. Harvey's father had owned it. Now it belonged to Harvey. His market had the freshest vegetables in the city.

Margaret opened the door to the market. Her face and hands felt cold from the outside. She took a small cart. "Hi, Harvey," she said. "How's your family?"

Harvey put down a big, heavy box. He turned to look at her.

"Fine, thanks. Margaret Kelly! You look so grown up. How are you?"

"Lonely," Margaret thought. But she didn't say that. Instead, she said, "I'm fine. We need some chicken and a few other things," she told him.

"There's some fresh chicken at the back of the store," Harvey said. And I just got some carrots in. Look around. Maybe you'll find something else."

"I've got a list," Margaret said. "I don't need anything else."

"Well," Harvey said, "sometimes the surprises are the best things."

Margaret went to the back of the store. She put a chicken into her cart. The chicken felt cold, just like the weather outside. She walked by the fresh breads. She checked the list. She didn't need any bread. She quickly rolled the cart away. There was another cart in front of her, but Margaret didn't see it. Her cart crashed into the other cart.

The man behind the other cart fell down. Margaret rushed over to him. He had short brown hair. His head was down. She stood over him.

"Are you OK?" she said.

He looked up. His eyes opened wide. It was Patrick.

"I'm so sorry," she said. She was embarrassed, but she was so happy to see him.

"It's OK," he said. He stood up. He brushed off his dark pants. He tried not to look at her, but he was so happy to see her. His heart was beating very quickly.

A Surprise Meeting

"Are you sure you're OK?" Margaret asked.

Some cheese had fallen out of the cart. Patrick picked it up.

"Let me help," Margaret said. She reached for the cheese, too. Their hands touched. Her stomach felt uneasy, like being in an airplane. She pulled her hand away.

"Sorry," they said at the same time.

"Have you . . . have you heard from Brendan?" she asked.

"Yes. You?"

"Yes," Margaret said.

Margaret didn't understand these feelings. She wanted to stop the feelings for Patrick, but the feelings wouldn't stop. She felt hurt because Patrick seemed so angry at her. "Well," she said, "I guess I'd better take this chicken home. My mom's waiting for me."

"Me, too," Patrick said. "I mean, I have to go."

Margaret rolled her cart away. Patrick watched her.

Margaret rushed back to her apartment. She gave the bag of food to her mother. She didn't even take off her jacket.

"Can you help me put it away?" her mother said.

Margaret quickly put the food away, then she said, "I've got to do something."

"Take off your jacket first," her mother said.

Margaret put her jacket on a chair in the kitchen. She rushed into the hall. She picked up the telephone.

Margaret called her best friend, Nancy Shaw. Nancy was a little older than Margaret. Nancy worked at a small newspaper. "Nancy, it's me, Margaret."

"Are you OK?"

"I saw him."

"Who?" Nancy asked.

"Patrick."

"Where?" Nancy said.

"At the market," Margaret said. Margaret shook her head. Her stomach felt sick again. "It was so good to see him."

"I'm worried about you," Nancy said. "What about Brendan? What are you going to do about Brendan? Don't you love him?"

"I do," Margaret said. Margaret touched the wall with her finger. "I think. I don't want to hurt him. But I don't want to hurt Patrick, either. What am I going to do?"

"Do you really want my advice?" Nancy said.

Margaret rested her back against the wall. "Yes, of course. You're my best friend," Margaret said. "I want your advice."

29

A Surprise Meeting

"Brendan loves you. He's a good man. He cares about you. Forget about Patrick," Nancy said.

* * *

The Caseys had just finished dinner. Patrick's father was sitting in his favorite chair in the living room. His feet were resting on the coffee table. He was listening to the radio. It was an old Irish program. He liked to listen to the radio. Sometimes he talked to the radio, like it was a person.

Patrick sat on the old sofa across from his father. "I have a friend," Patrick told his father. But his father didn't hear him. "Dad, this is important."

His father turned off the radio. His hands had cuts from the shipyard. He looked at Patrick. His eyes looked a little tired. "All right," his father said. "I'm listening."

"I have a friend," Patrick said. He pulled at the bottom of his T-shirt.

"What is it? What are you talking about? What friend?"

"My friend has a problem," Patrick said. "A big problem."

His father took a deep breath, then let it out. "Patrick, just get to the point," his father said.

Patrick thought about two things every day: Brendan and Margaret. "My friend is falling in love with his brother's girl," Patrick said. "What do you think about that? What should my friend do?"

Patrick's father let out another deep breath. He looked at Patrick for a long time. He took his feet off of the coffee table. "Feelings change," his father said. "Girls come and go. The love for a brother doesn't."

Chapter 9
Proms and Promises

Patrick lay on his bed in his room. He read Brendan's letter a third time:

Dear Patrick,
 Please do something for me. Margaret's prom is in a week. They've asked her to sing there, but she doesn't have a date. She doesn't want to go.
 It's her prom. And it's her big chance to sing. She can't miss it. She wants to sing so much.
 She's a wonderful singer. Would you please take her to the prom? You'd make her so happy. And you'd make me happy, too.
  All my love,
  Brendan

Patrick put his face in his hands. "I can't believe this," he thought. "Brendan is asking me to date Margaret. Of course, he doesn't know how I feel about her. If Brendan knew, what would he say?" Patrick wondered.

Patrick put the letter into his pocket. He went into the kitchen. He called Margaret's number.

"She's not here," Margaret's mother said. "She's at the park. She's watching her little cousin."

Patrick slowly walked to the park. A cool breeze blew in his hair. Birds were singing. Patrick put his hands into his pockets. He watched the trees. They were full of leaves. He loved the spring.

Margaret was on the sand. She was wearing blue pants, a blue sweater, white socks, and tennis shoes. She was sitting with a little dark-haired girl. They were making castles in the sand.

"My castle has 10 rooms," the little girl said.

"My castle only has five rooms," Margaret said.

"Why?" the little girl asked.

"I don't need a big castle," Margaret said.

"Everyone needs a big castle," the little girl said. "You put your dreams there."

"You must have a lot of dreams."

"Lots," the little girl said. "I want to be a doctor or a nurse or a teacher or a cook or a singer. I can't decide."

"Well," Margaret said, "you have lots of time."

The little girl sat on her castle. Margaret sat on her castle. They both laughed.

Patrick walked to them. "Hi," he said.

Margaret stood. She brushed off her pants.

"You looked like you were having fun," Patrick said.

The little girl went to play.

"I always have fun with her," Margaret said. "She's a great little girl."

The sun was strong. Patrick couldn't look at it. He watched the sand. "I need to show you something," he said.

He pulled the letter from his pocket and gave it to Margaret. She read it, then she looked up.

"We can't," she said.

Patrick looked at her. She looked so natural, so beautiful. "Are you supposed to sing?" he asked.

"Well, yes, but . . ."

"Then you have to go."

Margaret shook her head. "Look, you don't have to . . ."

"I want to. I don't want you to miss your prom."

"Do you think it's OK?" Margaret said. "I mean, is it OK for us to go together?"

"It's only so you can sing."

Proms and Promises

"Right," Margaret said. "Just to sing."
"We won't really be together," Patrick said.
"Of course not."
"It's not a big deal," Patrick said.
"No, it's not," Margaret said.
"All right," Patrick said. "I'll pick you up Friday at 7:00 P.M."
"All right."

* * *

Margaret and her sister, Molly, went shopping for a prom dress. They were in the tiny dressing room of Sarah's Dresses. It was a small dress shop near the center of Boston. Margaret had looked at many dresses. Finally she picked three dresses.

There was a mirror outside the dressing room. The first dress was a long white cotton dress. Margaret came out to see the dress in the mirror.

Molly was sitting on a chair, next to the mirror. She wore a straight brown skirt with a matching jacket. She wore a sweater under the jacket. "Too sweet-looking," Molly said. Molly had a strong face, like their father. Margaret had a small face with big dark eyes, like their mother.

"Don't I want to look sweet?" Margaret said.

"Not that sweet," Molly said. "A singer shouldn't look that sweet."

Margaret came out in another dress. This one was long, with little yellow flowers on it.

"You look like someone's garden," Molly said.

Margaret went back into the tiny room. She came out in a beautiful pink dress.

Margaret stopped at the mirror. Molly stood next to her. "That's it," Molly said. "Do you like it?"

"I love it," Margaret said. Margaret brushed her hand against the dress. The material was so smooth. "Molly?"

"What?" Molly said.

"Do you think it's OK? Should I go to the prom with Patrick? I mean, Brendan asked him to take me."

Molly put her hand on her sister's shoulder. "I thought I understood this. You have a chance to sing. You're going because you want to sing, that's all."

* * *

Patrick went into his father's bedroom. His father was sitting on the bed. He looked at Patrick.

"Dad?" Patrick said. "Can I borrow your suit?"

Patrick's father stood up. He walked to Patrick. They were the same size.

"Why do you need my suit?" his father said.

Patrick looked into his father's eyes. "I'm taking Margaret to her prom tomorrow night. Brendan asked me to take her."

His father put his hands into the air. "What?" he said. He was angry.

Patrick didn't understand why his father was so angry. "I got a letter from Brendan," Patrick said. "He wants me to take Margaret to the prom. She has to sing there. Can I borrow your suit?"

"You can't do that. That's your brother's girlfriend."

"He asked me to take her," Patrick said.

"Patrick, does Brendan know about you and Margaret?"

"Know what? What are you talking about? What about me and Margaret?" Patrick asked.

"I'm sorry. I mean your friend. The one you asked me about. The one who loves his brother's girlfriend."

"Was I that obvious?" Patrick asked.

"You've been walking around this house like a lost dog," his father said. "Listen, son, I understand how you feel. But think about Brendan. He trusted you with his girlfriend. What would Brendan do if he knew the situation?"

"He'd probably hit me in the face. But I can't explain the situation to Brendan right now. There's no time. And Margaret really wants to sing at her prom. I can control my feelings for Margaret."

"I can't tell you what to do, Patrick. You're 18 years old. You're a grown-up. If you want my suit, take it. But think about your brother. You're going to destroy your relationship with him."

Patrick's father left the room. Patrick stood at the closet and looked at the suit. He turned away. Then he went back to the closet. "I have to do this," he thought. "This is really important to Margaret. But that's it. After tonight, I won't see her again."

Chapter 10
Margaret's Song

There were hundreds of stars in the dark sky. Patrick and Margaret walked from his car to Margaret's high school. The school was in the old part of Boston, near a 100-year-old church. There were trees everywhere. A breeze was blowing through the trees.

Patrick stopped walking. He started to fix his tie before they went inside.

"Here," Margaret said. "Let me do that."

She stood close to him. She looked beautiful. Her hair was up. She fixed Patrick's tie. She felt his breath on her face.

They walked into the dance. It was very crowded. There were colored lights everywhere. There was a band. There was a big shiny dance floor in the middle of the room. Couples were dancing to a slow song. There was food in one corner. There were tables and chairs all over the room, like a restaurant.

Patrick felt Margaret's arm touch his. He looked at her from the side. He saw her small nose and her beautiful mouth. "Stop that," he thought. "She's Brendan's girl. We're here because Margaret wants to sing. That's it."

Margaret's Song

Patrick looked at the food on the table. "Are you hungry?" he asked.

"I'm always hungry," she said.

"Here," he said. He led her to a chair. "Why don't you wait here? I'll get you something to eat."

He went to the table. He saw meat, fish, sandwiches, vegetables, fruit, and creamy desserts. Patrick filled two plates with chicken, fish, cheese sandwiches, carrots, grapes, and chocolate cake. He walked back to Margaret.

Margaret looked at the plates. Each one had piles of food. "Is that enough?" she asked. She almost laughed.

"You said you were hungry."

They hardly spoke while they ate. Then Margaret went to say hello to someone on the dance floor. She looked around. She moved to the music. She obviously wanted to dance. But Patrick was afraid to touch her. "This wasn't a good idea," he thought. His father was right. "Control," Patrick thought. "She's Brendan's girl."

The band played another slow song.

A girl waved at Margaret. She wore a red-and-white dress.

"Patrick, this is Diane Washington. Diane, Patrick Casey."

"It's nice to meet you," Patrick said.

"Nice to meet you," Diane said. "Come on, you two, dance," she said to them.

Margaret looked at Patrick. She held out her hand. "I guess we can dance. This is a prom. That's what people do at a prom."

They danced to the music. Margaret felt very soft. Her hair and skin smelled like flowers. His heart was beating very quickly, but he was in control.

A girl with red hair and a long blue dress rushed over to Margaret. She touched Margaret's arm lightly. Margaret stopped dancing. "It's time for you to sing now, OK?" the girl said.

"Sure," Margaret said.

Patrick watched Margaret walk to the band. There were two male singers and a piano player. She stood next to the piano.

The light was shining in her eyes. She began to sing "Unforgettable." Patrick couldn't look away. The music changed her. Her face was soft, but her voice was strong. He listened to the words. "I can't forget her. I can't fight my feelings," he thought. Feelings of love rushed at him. He needed to tell Margaret, and soon.

She finished the song. The crowd went crazy. She rushed to him. "Was I OK?"

Margaret's Song

Patrick took her arm. "You were unforgettable," he said. "Come with me. I want to talk to you." They went outside, behind the building. He turned to her. "Margaret, I can't fight it any more. I love you." He took her in his arms and kissed her.

Margaret was surprised. "Patrick!" she cried. He stopped. She looked at his face. Then she put his face in her hands and kissed him again. "I love you, too," she said.

"I don't want you to sing for anyone else," Patrick said.

"What about Brendan?" she asked.

"We'll make him understand," Patrick said. "We'll make everyone understand."

Later that night, Patrick came home. His father was waiting in the dark living room.

"How was the dance?" his father asked.

Patrick couldn't look at him. He walked across the living room.

His father turned on the light. "How was the dance?" his father asked again. He put his hand on Patrick's shoulder. "I'm asking you a question," his father said.

"I don't know," Patrick said. He couldn't tell his father the truth. "The dance was fine," Patrick said.

His father let Patrick's arm go. "I knew it," his father said. Patrick's father didn't like to talk about feelings, but he understood them very well. He watched people, especially his sons. He didn't need words.

"What?" Patrick asked.

"You had to do it. You had to go to the dance. You knew your brother wouldn't approve. But you did it anyway. Now what are you going to tell Brendan?"

Patrick went to his room. He looked at Brendan's empty bed. He missed him, and he loved him.

"What *am* I going to tell Brendan," he thought. He took out a piece of paper. He started to write a letter to his brother. Finally, he wrote about all of his feelings for Margaret. "*Brendan, I never wanted to hurt you. I'm so sorry*," he wrote.

* * *

The next day, Margaret was sitting on the steps to her apartment building with Nancy Shaw. Margaret put her hand on Nancy's arm. "I feel terrible."

"Why?" Nancy said.

"Because I love him."

Nancy let out a deep breath. "Who?"

Margaret's Song

"Patrick," Margaret said.

"Patrick is a kid," Nancy said.

The mailman stopped in front of them and gave Margaret a letter. "This is for you," he said.

Margaret opened the letter. It was from Brendan. She read it to Nancy.

Dear Margaret,

I'm leaving Korea in two weeks. I'm finally coming home!

I have to ask you something. It's very important. The day I left for Korea, I made a promise to myself. If I didn't die in the war, I would ask you this: Margaret, will you marry me?"

Margaret put the letter into her pocket. She stood up. She felt like she was in a bad dream. She felt Nancy's hand on her back.

"Do you want my advice?" Nancy said.

"No," Margaret said.

"I'm going to give it to you anyway. I think you should marry Brendan. He's a good man. He loves you. I think you should forget about Patrick."

Margaret turned to Nancy. "There's only one problem," Margaret said. "I thought I loved Brendan. But I didn't know what love was. Now I know. And I love Patrick."

Margaret went into her apartment. She went to her room. She started to write a letter to Brendan. Finally she wrote about all of her feelings for Patrick: *"Brendan, I never wanted to hurt you. I'm so sorry."*

Chapter 11
Welcome Home

The bus station was crowded. Patrick's father wouldn't look at him. His father wore his suit. His mother wore her green dress, the one she always wore to church. She had a package of food with her. "Brendan might get hungry before we get home," she had said before they left.

Patrick wore a white shirt, a blue tie, and light blue pants.

"The welcome-home party is tonight," Patrick's father said. "You and Brendan have to act like brothers." It sounded like an order.

There were many young men coming home from the war. Other families were meeting their sons at the bus station. Everyone was hugging. Everyone looked so happy.

Another bus stopped. Patrick listened to the sound. Patrick's mother watched the bus carefully. The door of the bus opened, and lots of young men came out. Each one stopped and looked at the crowd. Then each man melted into the crowd.

Patrick finally saw Brendan step off the bus. He looked older and thinner.

Brendan didn't look at Patrick. He walked to his father and hugged him. His father looked like he was crying. Patrick had never seen him cry before. Then he hugged his mother. She was definitely crying.

39

Welcome Home

Finally, Brendan looked at Patrick, who was standing next to their father. Brendan wasn't smiling. "Hello," Brendan said softly to Patrick.

They got into the car. Patrick and Brendan sat in the back seat. Patrick couldn't look at his brother.

"Brendan, it's so good to have you home," Mr. Casey said. "Your mother and I have a surprise for you. It's a welcome-home party."

Brendan talked on the phone all day. At 5:30 P.M., Patrick went to the bathroom to take a shower. But Brendan was in the bathroom. Patrick opened the door, but Brendan slammed it in his face.

"Sorry," Patrick said.

Brendan came out of the bathroom. Patrick said, "Brendan, we need to talk." Brendan walked past him.

When Patrick finished his shower, he went into their bedroom. Brendan was wearing a white shirt and black pants.

Patrick took a green shirt from the closet. Brendan walked to the closet. He looked at his brother, then he looked at the shirt.

"That's my shirt," Brendan said.

Patrick looked at Brendan. Brendan's hair was still wet.

"You're crazy," Patrick said. "I wear that shirt every week."

Brendan shook his head. "It's still my shirt. You've been wearing my shirt. Mom gave it to me last year. Before I went to Korea."

Patrick put the shirt in the closet. Brendan was quiet. He looked at his brother. "Did you take everything I had? You took my shirt, you took my girlfriend. Did you take anything else? My shoes? My job at the shipyard? What about this party tonight . . . maybe it's for you instead of me."

"Brendan, stop it. I didn't want this to happen. I tried to explain." He walked over to Brendan. He stopped a few feet away from his brother.

Brendan put his jacket on. "I asked you to take care of my girlfriend. I said, 'Keep her away from other guys.' Well, you kept her away. You kept her for yourself. And now you want to explain!" He pulled out two letters from his jacket pocket and waved them in front of Patrick's face. One was from Patrick. The other was from Margaret.

"What do you want? Do you want me to say it's OK? It's not OK!" Brendan turned away from Patrick. He put the letters back into his pocket.

Brendan shook his head. "I trusted you!" he shouted.

"I'm sorry! I didn't want this to happen!" Patrick said.

"Then don't let it happen. Get away from my girlfriend!" Brendan

Welcome Home

yelled. His face was red. His hands were shaking.

Patrick didn't know what to say. "I never wanted to hurt Brendan," he thought. "But I can't leave Margaret. I love her." He put his hand on Brendan's shoulder.

Brendan slapped his hand away. "Don't touch me," Brendan said.

Brendan put on his shoes. He went into the living room to wait for his friends.

The Caseys invited all of Brendan's friends to the party. There was a lot of food on a table in the kitchen.

Brendan sat on the sofa, waiting. A big sign said: "Welcome Home." Brendan's mother sat next to him. She was still wearing her green dress. She smiled at him. Her dark eyes looked worried. "So," she said, "how are you and your brother doing?"

Brendan shook his head. He smiled. "Did you hear our fight?"

"It's a small apartment," she said. "Thin walls." She took his face in her hands. She smelled like flowers. "You can't fight with your brother," she said. "It isn't right."

The doorbell rang. His mother stood up. "Think about it, Son." She went to the door. Sam walked into the room. Brendan stood up.

"Sam! I didn't know you were back," Brendan said. "It's great to see you."

Soon the room filled with family and friends. Patrick felt terrible. He stayed in the kitchen. He didn't want to be near Brendan.

Jim walked into the kitchen. He saw Patrick. "Hey, what are you doing in here? The party's out there," Jim said.

The doorbell rang again. Brendan opened the door. Margaret stood there, waiting to come in. She wore a white dress with pink flowers. Her dark hair was in soft waves.

"Brendan!" she cried. "You're home. It's so good to see you!" She put her arms around his neck and hugged him. But Brendan barely touched her. He didn't feel happy to see her. "Hello, Margaret," he said. He was very serious. They walked into the living room. People around them stopped talking.

In the corner of the room, Rick spoke softly to Sam. "This should be interesting."

Brendan and Margaret went into Brendan's bedroom. "Brendan, we need to talk," she said.

"Yes, we do," Brendan said. Just then, the doorbell rang again. "But not right now. Today's a big day for me. A lot of people want to talk to me. And I don't really want to talk to you." Brendan went to answer the door.

Margaret walked into the kitchen. Patrick saw her. He was surprised. "Are you crazy? What are you doing here? You said you weren't coming!"

"I had to come," she said. "I had to see Brendan. I feel awful about this whole situation." She held Patrick's hand and looked into his eyes. "Patrick, please understand. This is difficult for everybody. But I need to spend some time with Brendan. I have to."

Patrick didn't understand. But he saw something in her eyes. "She has to do this. I can't stop her anyway." He looked at her again. "Do whatever you need to do."

Chapter 12
"I Never Wanted to Hurt You"

The next day, Brendan and Margaret met in the park. They walked together, but they didn't talk for a long time. "Maybe I shouldn't be angry," Brendan thought. "Maybe I should be understanding."

Brendan held her hand. "Margaret, I'm sorry about last night. I know this was hard for you," he said. "War is hard for everybody. I saw some things I never want to see again. I saw men die. And I did some things, too. I'm not proud of those things. Maybe you did some things, too. Maybe you're not proud of them."

She stopped him. "Brendan, please."

But he wouldn't stop. "Let me finish. We're together now. We can start again. You're perfect, Margaret. I've never met anyone like you. I can forget the past year if you can. Let's start over. Let's forget this whole year, this whole war."

Margaret stopped walking and looked at him. She wanted to be in love with him, but she didn't feel it. "Brendan, I'm not perfect," she said. "But I can't forget this past year. Too much has happened." She let

43

"I Never Wanted to Hurt You"

out a deep breath. Then she put her other hand on top of his hand.

"I didn't want any of this to happen. I tried so hard to stay away from him, but I couldn't. Then you asked him to take me to the prom. I'm in love with Patrick. I'm so sorry, Brendan."

Brendan took his hand away and started to run.

She ran after him. "Brendan, please wait," she said.

Brendan stopped running and sat on a large rock. Margaret came and sat next to him. A tear fell from her face to the ground. "I'm so sorry," she said. "Brendan, please don't hate me. I never wanted to hurt you."

* * *

Brendan came home. Patrick was in the living room, watching television. He looked up at Brendan, but Brendan didn't say a word to him. He went straight to his bedroom.

"He doesn't look happy," Patrick thought. "I wonder what that means. I have to talk to Margaret."

He called Margaret on the phone. "Margaret, it's me, Patrick," he said quietly. "What happened?"

"Let's not talk over the phone," she said. "Why don't you come over here?"

"OK, but tell me . . ."

She stopped him. "I'll tell you when you get here." She hung up.

Patrick looked at his feet. His shoes were in the bedroom. "Oh, boy," he thought. "I really don't want to go in there. But I can't go out without my shoes."

He walked quietly to the bedroom. Brendan was lying on his bed. He was looking at the wall. Patrick couldn't see his face.

Brendan heard his brother. He turned his face. There were tears in his eyes. "Get out!" he yelled at Patrick.

"It's my room, too," Patrick said. "Anyway, I won't stay. I just want my shoes."

Brendan went to the closet and took Patrick's shoes. "You want your shoes?" He opened the window and threw the shoes onto the street. "There. There are your shoes."

Patrick didn't say a word. He turned and went out of the apartment. He walked down the stairs to the street. He found his shoes and put them on. Then he walked over to Margaret's apartment.

Margaret opened the door. There were dark circles under her eyes. She wore a white shirt and gray pants.

"Hi," Patrick said. He was wearing brown pants and a jacket.

Margaret walked into the hall. Patrick followed her.

"I Never Wanted to Hurt You"

"So? What happened?" Patrick said.

Margaret looked at the ceiling. Then she looked at Patrick. "I told him."

"You told him what?"

"I'm in love with you."

Patrick let out a deep breath. He smiled. "Thank you, Margaret Kelly."

"Thank you for what?"

"Thank you for loving me."

Patrick put his arms around her. They kissed.

"I have an idea," she said.

"What?" he said.

"Why don't you marry me?" she said.

"I'm supposed to ask you," Patrick said.

"Does that mean you don't want to?" Margaret asked.

"I'll tell you at dinner," Patrick said.

* * *

That afternoon, Patrick went to a jewelry store. He looked at rings. They were all so expensive. He didn't have much money. But he had to buy a ring for Margaret.

"I want to buy a ring," he said to the salesman.

"What kind of ring?"

"I'm asking my girlfriend to marry me."

"Oh, an engagement ring."

"Yeah. An engagement ring." The words sounded funny to Patrick. "An engagement ring," he repeated.

"How much do you want to spend?" the salesman asked.

"I only have $50," Patrick said. "It's my high school graduation present."

The salesman smiled at him. "Well, you can't get a diamond ring for $50, but maybe we have something." He showed Patrick a plain gold ring.

"It's OK," Patrick said. "Do you have anything else?" Patrick looked at the other rings. He saw a ring with a small white stone.

"What about that one?" he asked.

"It's not a real diamond," the salesman said. "But it's very nice."

"How much is it?"

"Forty-five dollars."

"I'll take it."

* * *

"I Never Wanted to Hurt You"

* * *

The next day, Molly went to Margaret's bedroom. She opened the door. She looked inside. Margaret was still sleeping.

Molly went to the window. She pulled back the curtains. The sun filled the small room.

Margaret opened her eyes. She slowly sat up in bed.

"It's noon," Molly said. "Are you going to stay in bed all day?"

Margaret got out of bed. She walked to the window. When she was next to her sister, she held out her left hand. There was a small ring on her finger.

Molly's chin dropped. "Is that . . . ?"

"Yes," Margaret said. "I'm marrying Patrick." She put her hand at her side.

"But what about Brendan?" Molly said.

Margaret looked at the floor. "I told him the truth—I love Patrick."

* * *

Patrick was sleeping late, too. He and Margaret had stayed out late. He was tired. But Brendan wasn't tired. He made a lot of noise. Then he pushed Patrick's bed.

"Get up!" Brendan yelled.

"Go away," Patrick said. He was still trying to sleep.

"Get up," Brendan repeated.

Patrick opened his eyes and looked at his brother.

"What's wrong with you?" Patrick yelled. He looked at Brendan.

"You need to know something," Brendan said. "I'm going to fight for Margaret. If she can stop loving me, she can stop loving you, too."

"It's too late," Patrick said.

"What do you mean?"

"I asked her to marry me," Patrick said.

Brendan looked like Patrick had hit him. Brendan backed away from Patrick. "You what? When?"

"Last night," Patrick said.

Brendan sat on his bed.

"Brendan, I love you," Patrick said. He held out his hands. "I don't want to hurt you. But Margaret and I are in love. We can't stop it. We both tried. We can't. How do you stop loving someone?" Patrick asked.

"Like this!" Brendan shouted. "You're nothing to me! I will never speak to you again!" Brendan rushed to the door. When he got to the door, he turned to Patrick and said, "You're not my brother anymore!"